JUST BEING TED

T0383505

Buster Books

Edited by **JONNY LEIGHTON**

Designed by **JACK CLUCAS**

Cover design by **JOHN BIGWOOD**

For Neve and Isla - **LS**

First published in Great Britain in 2021 by Buster Books,
an imprint of Michael O'Mara Books Limited, 9 Lion Yard,
Tremadoc Road, London SW4 7NQ

W www.mombooks.com/buster   f Buster Books   🐦 @BusterBooks   📷 @buster_books

Text and illustrations © Lisa Sheehan 2021

A CIP catalogue record for this book is available from the British Library.

ISBN: 978-1-78055-702-1

3 5 7 9 10 8 6 4

This book was printed in August 2021 by Bell & Bain Limited,
303 Burnfield Road, Thornliebank, Glasgow,
G46 7UQ, United Kingdom.

Just Being Ted

Lisa Sheehan

TED THE DRAGON lived alone in a big house deep in the woods.
He spent his days making all sorts of wonderful creations,
from delicious cakes and colourful costumes
to beautiful drawings and paintings.

Ted loved where he lived,
but there was just one problem ...

He didn't like being alone.

"If only I had some friends to share my creations with," Ted sighed.

Every time he tried to play,
the other animals ran away.

His thoughtful gifts and friendly smile,
weren't enough to make them stay.

When Ted flew up to greet the birds, whirling through the sky, they flapped their wings and sped away, chirruping in fright.

And even when he baked a cake for the rabbits who lived next door,
they took one look at his smoky breath and screamed,

"Everyone is afraid of me," Ted would say.
"Whatever I do, I'll **NEVER** make friends."

One day, Ted went to town to buy some new paints,
cake decorations and materials from his favourite shop.
He wore his best disguise so that no one would be scared
when they saw a dragon walking down the street.

In the shop window, he saw a poster that read:

ANNUAL

BEARS'
Picnic Party

The last
Saturday of summer

HONEY · CAKES · BALLOONS
FUN & GAMES

BALLOONS

CAKE MIX

POM POMS

"A party!" Ted cried. "I wonder if the bears will let me come?"

"I doubt it," said the shopkeeper. "Picnic parties are for **BEARS ONLY!**"

"Hmm," Ted said, "there has to be a way."

On the walk home, Ted had an idea.

"I'll sew a bear costume and dress up for the day!" he said.
"I'll become Ted the Bear and have lots of fun and make lots of new friends."

So, Ted made an amazing costume and practised growling in the mirror ...

... climbing trees outside ...

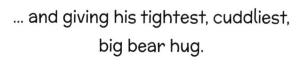

... and giving his tightest, cuddliest, big bear hug.

On the day of the party, Ted made his way through the woods and joined the queue of excited bears. When he got to the front, he handed over the invitation he'd made himself and put on his deepest, beariest voice.

"Can I come in, please?" he said.

The bear in charge took a long look at Ted.
"Of course!" he said. "What a big, fine bear you are.
Come on in, the party has just begun."

Ted was thrilled and skipped straight into the party. He played fun games, ate delicious food and, most importantly, made friends with the other bears.

He taught them how to make balloon animals and told jokes that made them laugh.
They thought he was the best bear they'd **EVER** met.

But after a while, Ted's costume began to feel a bit tight and he really wanted to stretch his wings.

Then, all the fizzy drink he'd had made him burp a huge cloud of smoke.

And when it was time for a big slice of honey
cake and the icing tickled his nose,
Ted couldn't help but let out a huge ...

As he sneezed, flames burst from his mouth and
his costume split into a hundred different pieces.
All the bears could see what he really was.

"He's no bear," they cried. "He's a **DRAGON!**"

Ted the Dragon picked up the pieces of his burnt costume.

"I think it's time I left," he whispered.

But as Ted turned to leave, a little bear
stepped forward. "Don't go yet ..."

"I'm not a bear, either," said a mouse, taking off
her costume. "I wanted to come to the party,
too, but no one ever notices us little mice."

Then, **ANOTHER** bear stepped
forward and took off his costume.
Underneath there was a moose.

"I'm always bumping into things
with my big antlers," he said.
"So I never get invited to parties."

Ted was so surprised.
He wasn't the only one
pretending to be something
that they weren't.

The bears weren't sure what to do. They'd never had other animals at their parties before. Some of them were a bit cross.

"Should we let them stay?"

"They aren't even bears!"

"I did like the dragon's balloons ..."

"... And the mouse and moose were fun!"

They talked it over in a big bear huddle, until they made a decision.

"We enjoyed having you here so much," they said, "that from now on
EVERYONE is welcome at the Bears' Picnic Party."

Ted was so pleased. Not only would he be able to go to the bears' big parties, he'd also made loads of new friends.

DRAGON RIDES

To celebrate, he took everyone out
for a special dragon ride through the sky.
He didn't have to wear a costume any more,
he was happy **JUST BEING TED**.

Although, every once in a while, he still liked to dress up ...